Carlos & Carmen

The Wobbly Wheels

by Kirsten McDonald
illustrated by Erika Meza

Calico Kid

An Imprint of Magic Wagon
abdopublishing.com

For the students and teachers at Emma Elementary School —KKM

This one is for Lucie - for being such an all-powerful superwoman! —EM

abdopublishing.com

Published by Magic Wagon, a division of ABDO, PO Box 398166, Minneapolis, Minnesota 55439. Copyright © 2017 by Abdo Consulting Group, Inc. International copyrights reserved in all countries. No part of this book may be reproduced in any form without written permission from the publisher. Calico Kid™ is a trademark and logo of Magic Wagon.

Printed in the United States of America, North Mankato, Minnesota.
052016
092016

THIS BOOK CONTAINS
RECYCLED MATERIALS

Written by Kirsten McDonald
Illustrated by Erika Meza
Edited by Heidi M.D. Elston
Designed by Candice Keimig

Library of Congress Cataloging-in-Publication Data

Names: McDonald, Kirsten, author. | Meza, Erika, illustrator.
Title: The wobbly wheels / by Kirsten McDonald ; illustrated by Erika Meza.
Description: Minneapolis, MN : Magic Wagon, [2017] | Series: Carlos & Carmen
  | Summary: The twins' father offers to teach them to ride their bikes without the training
  wheels--and with perseverance, and despite a lot of wobbling, the two soon succeed.
Identifiers: LCCN 2015045651 | ISBN 9781624021442 (print) | ISBN 9781680779592 (ebook)
Subjects: LCSH: Hispanic American families--Juvenile fiction. | Twins--Juvenile fiction. | Brothers
  and sisters--Juvenile fiction. | Bicycles--Juvenile fiction. | CYAC: Hispanic Americans--Fiction. |
  Family life--Fiction. | Twins--Fiction. | Brothers and sisters--Fiction. | Bicycles and bicycling--
  Fiction.
Classification: LCC PZ7.1.M4344 Wo 2016 | DDC 813.6--dc23
LC record available at http://lccn.loc.gov/2015045651

Table of Contents

Chapter 1
Leaves and Wheels

One warm Saturday morning,
Mamá and Papá were raking leaves.
Carlos and Carmen were pouncing
in the leaf piles.

Spooky was catching the leaves that fluttered down from the trees.

Papá leaned on his rake. He looked at the twins and said, "If you help with the leaves, I'll help you gemelos learn to ride your bikes."

"But we already know how," said Carlos.

"We can go really fast," added Carmen, kicking leaves into the air.

"Sí, but can you ride with just two wheels?" asked Papá.

"Not two wheels already!" said Mamá with alarm.

"Oh, Mamá," said Carmen. "We'll be fine. Right, Carlos?"

"Yo no sé," said Carlos slowly, reaching down to rub Spooky.

"You can show us first, right Papá?" asked Carmen.

Papá scrunched up his nose and said, "Not today."

Mamá rolled her eyes. She leaned her rake against a tree and said, "Let me go get the curitas."

Chapter 2
Getting Ready

Carlos and Carmen sat on the steps, putting on their helmets.

"Do you really think we can do this?" Carlos asked his sister.

"Sí, we're ready," said Carmen.

But Carlos was not sure. "What if I crash?" he said.

"You can crash in a leaf pile," Carmen told him.

"Yo no sé," said Carlos.

Carmen thought for a minute. Then she said, "You can do it, Carlos. I know you can. And Mamá and Papá will help."

"Are you ready, gemelos?" Papá asked.

Carlos looked at Carmen. Carmen looked at Carlos.

"Sí!" they said.

"Me too!" said Mamá, holding up the box of Band-Aids.

Chapter 3
Wobbling

"Me first," said Carmen. She sat on her bike seat with her feet on the ground.

Papá put one hand on the bike seat and one hand on the handlebar.

"¿Lista?" Papá asked Carmen.

"Ready!" answered Carmen.

"¡Vámonos!" said Papá. He ran, holding on to the bike.

Carmen pedaled.

Papá let go of the handlebar.

Carmen wobbled and pedaled.

Papá let go of the bike seat.

Carmen pedaled and wobbled.

"Look at me!" shouted Carmen.
"¡Mira!"

Then she wobbled once more and fell over into a big pile of leaves.

"Are you alright?" yelled Carlos.

Carmen stood up. She said, "Sí, but I'm feeling a little bit wobbly." Then she added with a little laugh, "But not as wobbly as when I was on my bicicleta."

"Okay, Carlos," said Papá. "It's your turn. ¡Vámonos!"

"Any advice?" Carlos asked Carmen.

"Pedal fast and hold on tight," she told her twin. She added, "Oh yeah, it's mucho mejor if you don't crash."

"Maybe you could show me how, Papá," said Carlos.

"Oh, no," said Papá. "I don't think I'll ride a bike today."

Carlos sat on his bike seat. He held the handlebars tightly.

Papá put one hand on the handlebar and one hand on the bike seat.

"¿Listo?" Papá asked Carlos.

"Maybe," said Carlos.

Carlos started to pedal.

Papá ran beside him holding on to the bike.

Carlos pedaled a little faster.

Papá let go of the handlebar.

Carlos pedaled faster, but he did not wobble.

Papá let go of the seat.

Carlos pedaled even faster.

"Look at me!" Carlos shouted. "¡Mira!"

Then he started to wobble. He wobbled to the left. He wobbled to the right. He wobbled off of the sidewalk and crashed into a giant pile of leaves.

Mamá ran toward Carlos, waving the box of Band-Aids. "Are you okay?" Mamá shouted.

Carlos stood up and brushed off the leaves. Then Carlos saw a little bit of red on his elbow and a little bit on his knee.

"Sí, I'm okay," said Carlos, still looking at his elbow. "But I might need some of your curitas, Mamá."

Chapter 4
On Two Wheels

For the rest of the morning, Carlos and Carmen wobbled a lot. And, they crashed a lot. But, they kept on trying.

Soon they could pedal fast. They could steer straight. And, they could ride without wobbling.

They pedaled back to Mamá and Papá. Mamá had her bike and her helmet.

Mamá said, "There's someone else who needs to learn to ride a bike."

Carlos said, "But you already know how to ride, Mamá."

Carlos and Carmen looked at each other. Then they looked at Papá.

"Oh no," said Papá.

"Oh yes," said Mamá.

"Oh boy!" said Carlos and Carmen.

"And we can help you," said
Carlos.

Papá laughed. He put on Mamá's
helmet and got on her bike.

Carlos and Carmen each put one
hand on the seat.

"¿Listo?" Carmen asked.

"Yo no sé," said Papá nervously.

Carlos and Carmen held on to
the bike seat. They ran holding
on as Papá pedaled and wobbled.

"Faster, Papá," shouted Carlos and
Carmen.

Papá pedaled a little faster, and
they let go. Papá pedaled even faster.
He did not wobble.

"Look at me!" he shouted. Then he
crashed into a big pile of leaves.

Mamá ran toward Papá, waving
the box of Band-Aids. She put one
Band-Aid on Papá's elbow and one on
his knee.

"Hooray, Papá," said Carlos. "Now
you can ride too."

"And I can crash too," said Papá.

"And, I think it's time for lunch,"
said Mamá.

Then the four of them walked back to their house. They all had smiles on their faces. They all had sparkles in their eyes. And, two of them had Band-Aids on their elbows and knees.

Spanish to English

bicicleta – bicycle

curitas – Band-Aids

gemelos – twins

¿Listo? / ¿Lista? – Ready?

Mamá – Mommy

¡Mira! – Look!

mucho mejor – much better

Papá – Daddy

sí – yes

¡Vámonos! – Let's go!

Yo no sé – I don't know